T0198905

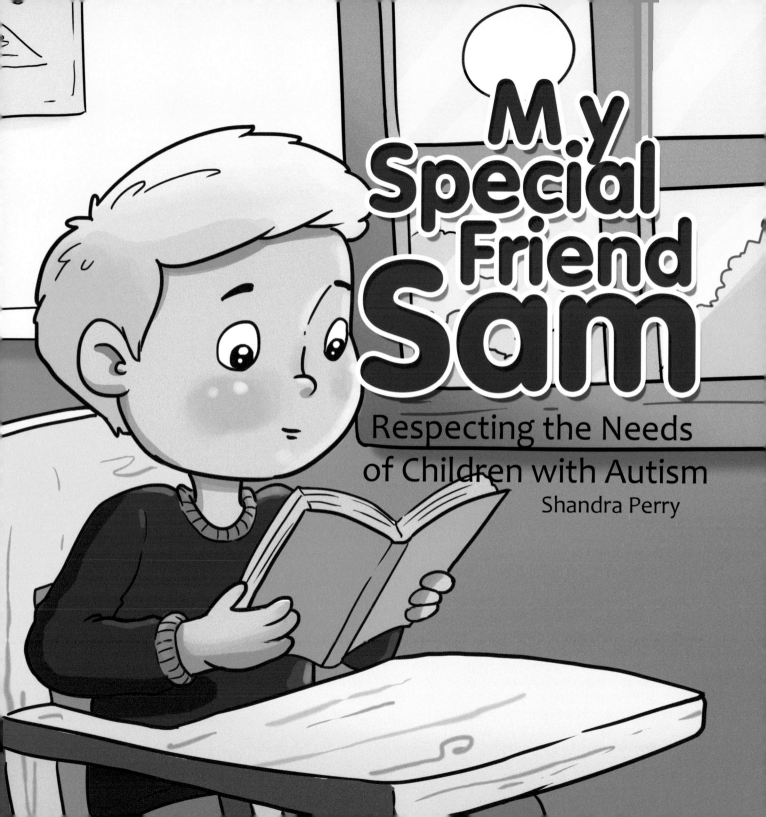

My Special Friend Sam

Respecting the Needs of Children with Autism

Shandra Perry

To order additional copies of this book, contact:
Xlibris
1-888-795-4274
www.Xlibris.com
Orders@Xlibris.com

MY SPECIAL FRIEND SAM

Subtitle: Respecting the needs of children with Autism

Dedication

To God. To children and the families
of those affected by Autism

Everybody say "Hi Sam"....Sam didn't even look!

Click

Click

Click

6

Sam is very busy, so if you need something you'd better say it quick.

Oh look! Sam found something more interesting and it goes click click click.

Sam doesn't like loud noises or touching gooey things.

And sometimes you can find him with zipped lips while the class sings.

Sometimes it can be hard for Sam
to say what's the matter.

His favorite spot is bouncing next to the teacher going "chatter chatter chatter."

"Sam! You can chew on this until its time for lunch."

Same likes to pretend that he is a jumping jellybean.

Now look at Sam as he dances to a tune like a jitterbug.

I love Sam the most because he gives the best hugs!

Printed in the United States
By Bookmasters